Grateful Jake

story by Emily Madill
artwork by Izabela Bzymek

I would like to extend a special thank you to Crystal Stranaghan for her talent, expertise and guidance on this project. Another special thank you goes to Izabela Bzymek for injecting an element of fun into the story and bringing the Grateful Jake characters to life in such a creative and extraordinary way. I am so grateful to have had the pleasure of working with both of you, thank you from the bottom of my heart.

Library and Archives Canada Cataloguing in Publication

Madill, Emily Elizabeth, 1978-
    Grateful Jake / Emily Madill & Izabela Bzymek.

Issued also in electronic format.
ISBN 978-0-9812579-7-6 (bound).--ISBN 978-0-9812579-6-9 (pbk.)

    1. Gratitude--Juvenile fiction. I. Bzymek, Izabela, 1979-
II. Title.

PS8626.A32G73 2012   jC813'.6   C2012-905037-7

This book printed in the USA on paper that contains no fibre from old-growth forests and using ink that is non-toxic and safe for children.

Grateful Jake is dedicated to Jake and Joe - two very special guys who inspire me to feel grateful each and every day.
Love Mom

Homework on a Friday? "Forget it!" Jake muttered to himself. He had big plans for the weekend, and making a list of 10 things he was grateful for was not on his agenda.

"What's so great about being an ordinary 8 year old boy anyway?" Jake thought.

"That's right – NOTHING !"

He crumpled up his homework page and tossed it in the garbage can beside his desk.

The first part of Jake's big plan was a bike ride with friends, followed by a game of soccer at the park across the street.

His team won **2** out of **3** games against the other neighbourhood kids, and Jake was worn out and starving by the time they were done.

PIZZA and

ICE CREAM

were definitely part of Jake's Friday Night game plan and he was in luck — they were part of his mom's plan too!

When it was time for bed, Jake's dad came in to read a story and say goodnight. He said he couldn't understand how any boy could sleep in a room with so much

MESS.

Jake replied, "It's okay Dad, I know where everything is".

Tomorrow will be a big day, thought Jake. Then he drifted off into a deep sleep.

The next morning Jake was feeling rested and full of energy. He raced out to his garden box to fill his bucket with tasty treats.

After a delicious breakfast of **ripe strawberries** Jake was content and cheerful. Next stop – beachcombing!

Jake and his big brother Joe tip-toed over rocks covered with

SLIPPERY SEAWEED.

They saw colourful starfish in tide pools and hundreds of oyster shells and clam shells scattered about the beach.

With their buckets full of shiny rocks and rare seashells, the boys climbed up the steep path to their backyard.

After Jake added his new treasures to his collection,
his mom said they were packed and ready to go.
He hopped in the car and
they drove to the lake
for a swim and a
PICNIC
LUNCH.

Jake had a wonderful time SPLASHING and playing around with his family in the water.

Later, Jake's mom suggested the boys go play at the park.
Jake was happy to see his friends Matthew and Rebecca.
They played a game of HIDE AND SEEK
with Joe and some of the bigger kids.

Jake and his friends
knew a few tricks even the
older kids didn't figure out!

The next day Jake helped his mom in the garden and found a few new bugs to add to his bug jar. He tasted a handful of juicy strawberries and munched on some sweet peas before he got to work weeding. While he was digging out weeds from between the carrot tops, Jake found a long earth worm.

He let the slimy worm wriggle through his fingers before releasing it into the thick blades of wet grass.

That afternoon was really **HOT**, and Jake had fun soaking Dad with the hose while they washed the car.

The soap suds collected between Jake's toes so he sprayed the **cool** water over his warm feet and then took a few slurps from the hose to quench his thirst.

At dinner that night, Mom asked what everyone's favorite part of the weekend was.

Jake said, "It was the bike ride, ah no- the fun with friends, um no- the pizza night, er no - my strawberries, or the beachcombing, and the lake, or the..."

Jake's eyes opened **VERY WIDE** and he ran to his room.

Jake rummaged through his garbage until he found the crumpled up homework assignment.

Being grateful was feeling thankful for things he liked to do, that were fun and made him feel good. This homework assignment was going to be a breeze!

Jake filled out 10 things on his list with no trouble at all, and then he hurried back downstairs to see if he could fit even more fun into his weekend!

About the author

Emily lives on Vancouver Island, BC with her husband and two sons. She has a degree in Business and Psychology. Emily believes in the importance of teaching children accountability and empowerment from a young age. She enjoys writing and creating anything that will inspire others to believe in themselves. Being a mother is the most creative job she has had to date.

Books by this author:

Captain Joe to the Rescue! (paperback)
Captain Joe Saves the Day! (paperback)
Captain Joe's Gift! (paperback)
Captain Joe's Choice (paperback)
The Captain Joe Collection (hardcover)
Captain Joe Teaching Resources (paperback)

Grateful Jake (paperback)
Grateful Jake (hardcover)
Grateful Jake (iPad edition with audio)
Grateful Jake Resource Guide (paperback)
Grateful Jake Resource Guide (iPad edition)

Emily's books are available for purchase through her distributor Red Tuque Books, and from online sellers such as Amazon around the world.

For more information visit www.emilymadill.com

iPad editions

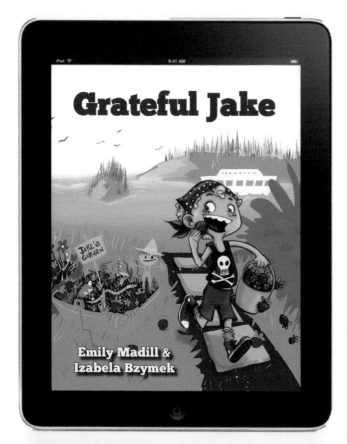

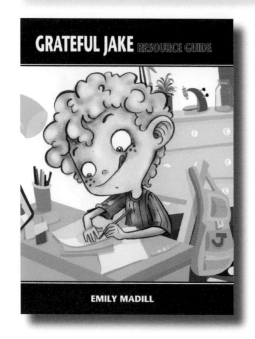

Grateful Jake Resource Guide is perfect for solidifying children's awareness and practice of gratitude and encouraging them to begin developing an 'Attitude of Gratitude'. Suitable for classroom use, home schooling or to have some fun activities to do together as a family!

The guide includes:
* 12 different lesson plans based on the Grateful Jake Book including a variety of handouts to complement the lessons
* Additional resources, including a Math Worksheet, Word Search, Vocabulary list, and Story Sequence handout
* Comprehension, Word Study and Critical Thinking worksheets
* Colouring Sheets

About the Captain Joe Series

The Captain Joe Series was designed as a tool for adults to teach children about constructive imagination. The four books are a fun and interactive way to introduce the concept of "Thoughts Turn Into Things" (so choose the ones that make you happy) to young children, ages five to nine years.

Joe and his thought-zapping superpower will invite children to use their imaginations to constructively choose thoughts that promote healthy self-esteem and self-awareness. Each story is designed to teach a key concept.

CAPTAIN JOE TEACHING RESOURCES

EMILY MADILL

- Captain Joe to the Rescue is a great way to begin discussions with children around thoughts, attitudes and personal power in shaping them.

- Captain Joe Saves the Day is a great way to open discussions around the importance of following our dreams in an appealing way kids will relate to.

- Captain Joe's Gift is a great way to introduce discussions with children around standing up against bullying and celebrating our differences.

- Captain Joe's Choice is a great introduction to discussions around the power of our thoughts and choices in creating our happiness.

- Captain Joe Teaching Resources contains 100+ pages of lesson plans, worksheets and ideas to help parents and teachers extend learning based on all 4 Captain Joe books in the series.

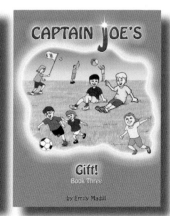
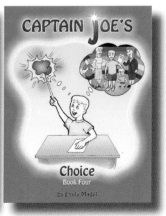

Printed in Great Britain
by Amazon